the REAL

facts of life

You might think that facts of life are hard to find but they're everywhere — all the time. Mostly people just don't see them, even when they're obvious. I do though. I see all.

Take last weekend for instance. Now there was a weekend busting with facts. I collected heaps. But I missed the most amazing one of all. I can't believe I didn't see it coming. It was obvious when I look back. Look, I'll tell you the whole story, but I'd better start at the beginning …

Geoff Havel was born in the mountains of New Guinea. As a baby, he liked to sit in a sandpit on the edge of the jungle, stuffing whole bananas down his throat. His manners have improved since then, that is, unless he spots a good idea for a story go past. Right in the middle of whatever he's doing he gets a faraway look in his eyes, rips out his trusty notebook and slams the idea between the pages.

Geoff has written two picture books, *Ca-a-r Ca-a-r* (1996) and *Punzie, ICQ!* (1999). These days he lives in Perth with his wife Sindy and two quickly growing children, Jade and Joshua. He teaches in a primary school where he and his class write lots of interesting stories that they read to each other.

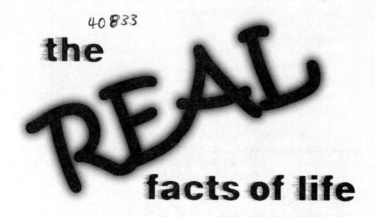

the REAL

facts of life

GEOFF HAVEL
ILLUSTRATED BY SHANE THOLEN

FREMANTLE ARTS CENTRE PRESS

First published 2001 by
FREMANTLE ARTS CENTRE PRESS
25 Quarry Street, Fremantle
(PO Box 158, North Fremantle 6159)
Western Australia.
www.facp.iinet.net.au

Consultant Editor Jane Hammond Foster.
Production Coordinator Cate Sutherland.
Designed by Brown Cow Design.
Typeset by Fremantle Arts Centre Press.
Printed by Griffin Press.

National Library of Australia
Cataloguing-in-publication data

Havel, Geoff, 1955– .
The real facts of life.

ISBN 1 86368 321 6.

I. Title.

A823.3

The State of Western Australia has made an investment in this project
through ArtsWA in association with the Lotteries Commission.

For
Mum and Dad

See — I was paying attention!

Acknowledgements

I must thank the children of Kinross Primary School who let me know the difference between opinion and fact. They are a continual source of inspiration.

I'd also like to thank Meg Worby, Jacinta di Mase, Jenny Darling, Clive Newman and Ray Coffey for seeing merit in this story and for helping me to finetune it.

Finally, to David, Lilliana, Romie, Tony, Glyn, Raewyn and all the other children's authors who let me bounce ideas off them, thanks heaps.

Ask Your Father

You know how it is when you're a kid. You ask your mum where babies come from and she looks surprised.

Then she says, 'From their mother's tummy.'

You say, 'How do they get in there?' And your mum looks even more surprised.

Then she says, 'Um ... um ...' and she goes red. 'Ask your father.'

So you ask your dad. He looks surprised.

Then he says, 'From their mother's tummy.'

You say, 'That's what Mum said, but how did they get in there?'

Dad says, 'What brought this on? Have you been learning about the birds and the bees at school?'

Birds and bees? What on earth have birds and bees got to do with babies?

'Well, I guess it's time you learned about the Facts of Life. I have to go to work now, Max, but this afternoon

Mum and I will tell you everything you want to know,' Dad says.

Everything? Facts of Life? Well, I know a few facts of life myself. I've been collecting facts for ages. I've even got a notebook where I write them down. My friends reckon it's a bit weird. They started calling me 'Actual Factual'. I didn't mind that at all and after a while it got shortened to 'Factual'. I reckon it's even better — sort of cool — except when my stupid older sister Jess changes it to Factso, just to annoy me.

Anyway, I've got hundreds of facts now — a huge list of them I've collected over the last few months, like:

- **Fathers always read in the toilet.**
- **Being sick is only worth it on school days.**
- **When you have a hose you have to squirt someone.**
- **Older sisters think that they're smarter than you are — but they're not.**

You might think that facts of life are hard to find but they're everywhere — all the time. Mostly people just don't see them, even when they're obvious. I do though. I see all — unlike Jess, who thinks she knows everything, but usually doesn't have a clue.

Take last weekend for instance. Now there was a weekend busting with facts. I collected heaps. But I *missed the most amazing one of all. I can't believe I didn't see it coming. It was obvious when I look back. Look, I'll tell you the whole story, but I'd better start at the beginning.*

Weekend Facts

I think a weekend really begins when the bell goes for the end of school on Friday.

Actually, that's a fact. Here it is in my notebook.

FACT — Weekends start straight after school on Fridays.

At least they should! This is what really happened last Friday.

Five minutes before the bell went Ms Sluggitt told us to clean up, just like she always does.

This probably isn't a fact, but it's a rule I like to obey:

It's not my job to clean up someone else's mess.

So obeying this rule, I pushed anything that I didn't want onto Tony's desk. He pushed it back with an extra maths book and some paper. I pushed the lot onto Jane's desk. She got mad and shoved them back onto my desk. I was pushing it all back against her when they fell onto the floor.

Then Ms Sluggitt growled, 'What do you three think you are doing?'

'Nothing, Miss,' we all said, but she didn't believe us.

'That's the trouble,' she snapped. 'You're supposed to be cleaning up! Look at your desks. They look like World War Nine!' She looked grimly around the room. 'No one leaves until the room is tidy.'

And that's how we always waste the first five minutes of every weekend. We were all busting to get out, but all the other numbnuts kept talking and messing around. Kids from other rooms were walking past the windows with their bags over their shoulders and we were still standing there.

Finally, even Bill and Jane stopped talking and Joanna stopped giggling.

FACT — The weekend starts five minutes after the end of school on Friday — thanks to all the other kids.

Well, after we'd cleaned up, Ms Sluggitt stood there for a moment, making out she wasn't worried if we spent the whole weekend in the classroom, before she finally let us go. Then she finally said quietly, 'All right …' But, before she could finish, we charged for the door like a herd of wild animals.

Freedom at last! A whole weekend! It seemed to stretch out forever. I stood on the verandah sucking in the fresh air before I bolted for the crosswalk. There was time to do a million things, anything at all, but have you ever noticed that it seems like the weekend is already over before you even get started?

It's a fact:

FACT — Weekends and holidays go faster than school days.

Anyway, there I was heading home, the whole weekend ahead of me and just one tiny bit of maths homework to do. No worries, plenty of time to do it.

Fat chance!

I knew I'd end up doing it on Sunday evening when I really wanted to watch TV because a really good movie is usually on.

I went home and wasted a couple of hours watching a boring re-run kid's show on TV that I didn't really want to see anyway. 'Plenty of time,' I thought.

It's unbelievable! I do it every time. I know the facts but I just can't help myself. What's worse, Jess does her homework straightaway. It's like she does it on purpose just to annoy me. She reckons she's so smart, just because she's one year older than I am. So what! Eleven isn't that much older than ten, especially when you're dumb like she is.

Here's something that Jess probably hasn't figured out yet:

FACT — Teachers plan it so that homework is due the day after the best movies are on.

I think they sit up there in the staffroom with a TV timetable and a calendar. First they find all the best movies and they mark them on the calendar, then they plan the homework. When they have ruined my chances of ever seeing a good movie, they make a cup of coffee and laugh their heads off. It gives me the shivers thinking about Ms Sluggitt cackling away. Gruesome!

Anyway, I lay there in front of the TV, bored mindless while Goody-two-shoes Jess did her homework in no time at all. I was just about to get into an argument with her for being so annoying when Dad came home. He called Ms-She's-so-Good-it-Makes-You-Chuck Jess and me to one side and said that Mum needed to put her feet up. Then he gave Mum a great big hug and a kiss. I wondered what was up. Maybe he was trying to con something out of her. He isn't usually so soppy.

I looked across at Jess, and she gave me one of those 'I know something you don't know' looks. I can't stand it when something is going on and I don't know what it is, especially if Jess knows — or pretends she does. I would have to use all my powers of observation to figure this one out.

First Clue: Dad was being extra nice to Mum.

I was watching Mum and Dad closely when Dad said we were going out for takeaways. Yes!! And off we went.

Takeaway Facts

We pulled up at the drive-through speaker.

'How are you this evening?' said the speaker.

'How the heck does she know we're here?' I thought. I looked at the speaker and then the ground. Nothing! I looked all around the building. Nothing! She was around the corner out of sight; so how?

Fact — The people who talk on drive-through speakers have X-ray eyes.

'Stupendous! Absolutely fabulous!' Dad said to the speaker, giving Mum a wink. Mum just shook her head and looked away, but he didn't care. It just made him enjoy it even more. He squeezed Mum's knee and made her jump.

Anyway, the speaker was silent for a while. I was laughing because it was funny but Jess just looked embarrassed. Finally the speaker asked flatly, 'Are you ready to order yet?'

Dad started to order when Mum said, 'Just a minute, I think I'll have something different.'

Every time we go to a drive-through burger place the same thing happens. Dad tries to get us organised beforehand, but we always change our minds just as he is ordering and he can't stand it. He gets really mad. But this time he didn't say anything. That was unusual, but I didn't think much of it at the time. Jess and I were too busy yelling out what we wanted.

Second Clue: Dad was being patient when usually he freaks.

Then Mum said, 'Do you think these burgers have any listeria in them?'

Dad shook his head. 'The food's all fresh,' he said. 'It's only salami and things like that you have to worry about.'

'Ah!' said Mum and went back to making up her mind.

I wondered what listeria was. If it was in salami, how come I had some in my lunch today? How could salami be bad for her and not bad for us?

Third Clue: Mum was being really weird about burgers.

Mum kept thinking while Dad tapped his fingers on the steering wheel and looked in the rear-view mirror. There was a line of cars starting to build up and then the speaker asked if we were ready to order — again.

'Well?' snapped Dad. Mum still didn't know and Jess and I kept yelling our orders at the same time until finally Dad freaked out and ordered the same four burgers and chips we always get.

Fact — When you go to a drive-through, you always change your mind at the last minute — and then your dad freaks.

All the way home Mum sat silently and Dad stared straight forward. As we turned into our street Dad said, 'I wanted to make the evening relaxing for you.'

'I know, Dear,' said Mum, and squeezed Dad's knee. He jumped; Mum quietly grinned.

Dad trying so hard to be nice to Mum should have got me thinking a lot harder. The good thing was Jess hadn't noticed anything strange was going on.

We pulled up in the driveway and Jess and I

raced for the front door. Jess got there first, but I dragged her back. I got through the doorway before her and told her the winner was first one inside.

She just shrugged and said, 'What winner? We weren't having a race!' Then she pushed past me and sat at the dinner table.

Before I could think of some smart reply, Mum and Dad came in — luckily for Jess-oh-I'm-so-Smart-Knickers.

I bit into my burger and juice squirted out the back, ran down my arms and dripped all over my jumper. It tasted like soggy breakfast cereal mixed with tomato sauce and pickles. Yum!

Fact — Burgers always leak juice everywhere — no matter how careful you are.

Parent Facts

After dinner we spent a few fun family hours watching television. Dad watched the news on Channel 9, then he turned to Channel 7. When the ads come on he uses the remote to flick from channel to channel. He hates the ads so he surfs the stations.

Fact — Dads think they own the remote.

Fact — Dads drive you nuts by surfing the channels till they find another boring news program

Anyway, Mum, Jess and I were getting mad. He changed the channel so often we couldn't even watch the good ads. When he tried to watch the news on Channel 2 Mum put her foot down and we got to watch *Home and Away* instead.

Dad told Mum to put her feet up while he made her a cup made of tea. Something was definitely going on. He never does that! I looked across at Jess. She hadn't noticed. Excellent!

Fourth Clue: Mum has to put her feet up.

Then Mum went to sleep.

FACT — Television programs make adults go to sleep — unless it's the news.

With my parents, the TV on switch is like their off switch. Turn it on and their heads drop onto their chests. Turn it off and they wake up again.

Dad couldn't stand *Home and Away* for long so he went to the toilet with something to read. Truth is, he never goes to the toilet without something to read.

FACT — Dads always read in the toilet — for ages and ages.

When anyone else wants to use the toilet he yells out things like, 'I can't even get any peace in my own dunny!' (Like it's his own personal dunny!) And, 'I only just get in here and you kids start banging on the door.' (Yeah, like he's only been in there about two hours and everyone else is outside really busting!)

As usual, when the movie was about to start Mum and Dad decided it was bedtime. Jess and I complained that it was too early. Jess said that we didn't have to go to school in the morning, but it didn't work.

It is a fact:

FACT — Parents make you go to bed just when interesting things start happening.

And you know what? Jess and I have probably used up all the good excuses for staying up longer and my parents just get mad when we try to use them again. They tell us that they were kids once and they know exactly what we're up to.

FACT — Parents will get mad if you keep using these excuses:
1. *I'm just getting a drink.*
2. *I need to go to the toilet.*
3. *I just want to tell you something.*
4. *I didn't hear you say go to bed.*
5. *I feel sick.*
6. *I can't get to sleep.*
7. *I just want to give you a hug,*

Anyway, on Friday I tried to use excuse three.

'I just want to tell you something.'

'What?' growled Dad.

'Something,' I said.

'Tell me what?' Dad insisted.

'I want to tell Mum,' I said.

'Tell her then!' Dad snapped impatiently.

'Um,' I stalled. 'Um …' I waited until he was about to go ballistic and then I said, 'I forgot.'

He went ballistic anyway, but I did get to see a little bit of the movie. It was just some soppy love story.

After they made me get back in bed I heard Jess try to use excuse 7, but they were onto her. 'Just settle down!' shouted Dad, and that was that.

I lay there for a while thinking how unfair parents are and straining my ears to hear what was happening in the movie. It kept going too quiet for me to hear so I tried to figure out what was going on with Dad and Mum. I didn't work anything out before I went to sleep

In The Dark Facts

I woke up busting to go to the toilet. This was lucky because it meant I hadn't wet my bed.

FACT — If you pee in your dreams you are in big trouble.

There I was, lying in bed, busting, and I just knew that something was there, in the dark. Dad and Mum have told me that monsters don't exist but I was sure something was there. It might have been Dracula or a mad axe murderer, or just some plain, ordinary monster.

FACT — There might be monsters in the dark.

I couldn't quite see them but they might just have been there, in the dark corner by the wardrobe, or under the bed. Luckily I knew that monsters can't get you if you act brave, and anyway if the light is on they have to disappear and hide. So here are two more really useful facts:

FACT — Monsters can't get you if you act brave.

FACT — You are safe in the light.

I reached up to my bedside light and turned it on. There was a flash of light, then the globe blew. Dark again! What could I do now? It was darker than it had been before.

I lay in bed for ages hoping the need to pee would go away but it didn't. Just when I was about to blow from the pressure I acted brave and calmly walked to the light switch at the door. I was really terrified but I pretended I wasn't worried because I know another fact.

FACT — Monsters can't get you if you walk.

Once the light was on I was safe. Out in the hallway it was safe down my end because of the light but the other end was dark. Well, I just acted brave and walked to the toilet light switch and then the light kept me safe while I went.

What a relief!

Now the problem was I had to go back to my bedroom once I'd turned out the toilet light.

I turned the light off, acted brave, and walked the first bit, but about halfway down I started to walk quicker, and quicker, *and quicker* until I ran to the bedroom. My heart was beating like a drum in a rock-and-roll band, but at least I was safe in the light!

Now there was the problem of getting into bed after I turned out the light. Once I got under the covers I would be safe. That is another fact.

FACT — You are safe under the covers.

I had no choice. All I could do was turn off the light and dive for the bed. So I turned the light off and took a flying leap. My aim was good. I dragged the covers over my head and only left a tiny breathing hole.

As I lay there I heard Jess turn her light on and walk down the passage to the toilet. Here was my chance to scare her witless. Too perfect! I jumped up and crept down the passage to the toilet door. I scratched softly on it.

'Who's there?' Jess asked. 'Is that you, Factso?'

She sounded scared. I waited a few seconds and scratched on the door again.

'It's not funny, Factso!' Her voice was quavering a bit. Wicked!

FACT — You feel braver if you are scaring someone else.

I crept to the bathroom halfway down the hallway and waited. After a couple of minutes the toilet door opened. I couldn't see Jess's face because she would see me too but I imagined how scared she must look. It was hard not to laugh.

FACT — The more important it is not to laugh, the harder it is to hold it in.

I waited until she was close enough to me, then I quietly stepped out into the light.

Jess rose about a metre into the air. Her arms moved in little circles one way and her feet spun around the other way. Her eyes were wide and staring and out of her mouth came the most almighty scream. It scared me and I yelled back. That made her scream again.

'What's going on?' growled Dad from the end of the passage. 'What's all the noise about?' His hair stuck up all over the place like a weird flat-top.

'Nothing!' I said in my most innocent voice.

Dad looked at me like he didn't believe me and then, as usual, Jess dobbed on me. I got busted, but as Dad turned out the light after he made me go to bed I saw him grinning to himself. He thought it was funny too. Cool!

Saturday Morning Facts

Next morning, because it was the weekend, I woke up at sunrise and sprang out of bed feeling full of energy. On school days I feel like a flat tyre.

FACT — It is much easier to get up on weekends than on school days.

That is unless you're a parent. You should see Mum and Dad in the morning. Their faces need ironing. It's amazing what a shower does for them.

FACT — Showers make parents' skin shrink a bit and it stretches out some of the wrinkles.

I snuck down to the kitchen for breakfast. I

carefully opened the drawer to get a spoon out. There was a microscopic little rattle of one spoon on another and Dad yelled out, 'BE QUIET! YOUR MOTHER'S TRYING TO SLEEP IN!'

Duh! Like my little clink would do more to wake Mum than his giant roar.

FACT — Parent hearing is sharper on Saturday mornings.

And, it usually takes a bomb to wake Dad on a weekday.

But, the next thing I knew, for the first time in living memory, Dad got up and made Mum breakfast in bed.

Fifth Clue: Mum was getting breakfast in bed, and it wasn't even her birthday.

Dad said she was feeling a bit sick. I hoped it wasn't the flu or something horrible like that. Dad does all the cooking when Mum is sick and he puts too much onion in everything.

Cake Mix Facts

When Mum finally got up she seemed fine and decided to bake a cake. She likes to bake cakes on Saturdays.

I'm sure she knows how much it tortures me to see all that cake mix and know I can't have any. Here are some facts about cake baking.

FACT — Cake mix always tastes better before it is cooked.

FACT — Parents will not let you dip a spoon, or even just your little finger, into the mix.

FACT — There is never enough mix left on the beater.

It drives me mad.

'Mum, can I have some of that?' I asked hopefully.

I already knew the answer. Mum didn't even think before she told me I couldn't have any. It's automatic.

'If I give you some now there won't be enough to bake. You can lick the bowl if you like.'

Yeah, big deal — like the tiny bit in the bowl would satisfy me!

Over the years I have developed ways of getting my share of cake mix. Here are some hints you might like to use:

1. *Beg and beg and beg and beg.*

Trouble is this just annoys my mum now.

2. *Walk past acting innocent and scoop out some with your finger when no one's looking.*

This used to work but Mum is ready for me now. Mums are like detectives so you'll only get away with it once or twice.

FACT — You will be caught.

No matter how hard you try to smooth over the mark, your mum will spot it and you will be busted. It's true you get to taste a little cake mix but it's much better to try hints 3 and 4.

3. *Try to do a deal like — 'If I have a spoonful now I won't eat so much cake later when it's cooked.'*

Now that one really seems fair all round, but for some reason it hasn't worked yet.

4. *Volunteer to cook a cake yourself so you can sample all you like.*

Jess does this all the time and then she makes great big slurping and smacking lip noises while you watch her guzzling down the cake mix. Gross!

Unfortunately, yet again, for some reason, Jess volunteered to help Mum before I did so I couldn't use the cooking myself plan to get some of the mix. Begging and begging didn't work so I tried to steal some. I pretended I was going to get a drink and as I walked past I stuck my finger in the mix.

'Mum!' Jess yelled, pointing at me.

Mum turned around and caught me with my finger stuck up to the knuckle in my mouth. She looked at me and then at the bowl. Her eyes went squinty when she saw the gouge mark in the mixture.

'He pinched some,' dobbed my sister in her best 'punish him' voice.

Mum looked at the cake mix all around Jess's mouth where she had been sampling and looked back at me. I expected to be busted but Mum took out a spoon and gave me a dollop of mix. 'That's all you get!' she said. I was speechless. Mum never does that. I should have noted it down then, but I was too busy eating the cake mix.

Sixth Clue: Mum was giving away cake mix!!

'Muumm!' whined Jess, still trying to get me into trouble, but Mum just reminded her how much mix she'd had and told her to give it up.

Sisters are like that — dobbers.

FACT — Sisters always try to get you into trouble.

FACT — Sisters are annoying — even more of a pain than not getting any cake mix.

After Mum and Jess finished baking, there were dirty dishes everywhere. Dad said Jess (the mega-pain) and I had to do them.

Here is where the same principle I use for cleaning up at school applies at home.

Possible fact:

It is always someone else's turn to clean up.

The main problem with this is that my sister has the same principle when it comes to dishes. I figure that girls, especially older sisters, should do all the work and it's the boy's job to get out of as much work as possible. Now that should be a fact, in fact.

I said that Jess made the dishes dirty so she should clean them up. That didn't work. Mum said Jess had been helping her. So then I said it was Jess's turn anyway, but Jess said it was mine. Mum asked who did it the last time. We both said, 'Me!'

For some reason she didn't believe us and then she went and got that rotten roster. As usual it said that Jess did it last time and it was my turn today.

Thanks to the rotten roster I had to do the dishes — literally millions of them. I bet Jess made as many dirty dishes as she could because she knew I had to do them. That's loving sisters for you.

Have you ever noticed how dishes multiply?

Even more amazingly, once you start washing dishes, people keep finding more. If you have visitors, dishes begin to breed like rabbits. Say you have three visitors, then you will end up with enough dishes for six people.

FACT — There are always more dishes to wash than you used.

While I washed, Mum went around like a

lunatic cleaner. Every speck of dust drove her crazy. She buzzed around the house like a bee in a bottle, cleaning anything that stood still for too long.

What's worse she made us help, for ages and ages. She wasn't wearing any white gloves to test for dust but it was nearly that bad. She cleaned this and then that and then this again. But when she started getting all sniffly because a germ might have escaped, Dad made her lie down.

I'd never seen Mum get so worked up about the house before. There weren't even visitors coming, so it was weird.

Seventh Clue: Mum was acting like a lunatic cleaner.

Sister Facts

That afternoon, Dad asked Jess and me to be quiet while Mum slept. It was the perfect sort of afternoon for brothers and sisters to get each other into trouble.

FACT — Brothers and sisters always try to get each other into trouble — but somehow sisters, especially older sisters, seem to be better at it.

I went into my bedroom and innocently lay down with one of Dad's surfing magazines.

'Dad,' whined Jess, 'Factso has got one of your magazines.' She gave me a triumphant sort of look.

FACT — Sisters always dob in really whiney voices.

'Quiet!' hissed Dad from the lounge. 'Mum's asleep!'

I heard him get up and come to the door.

'Which one?' he asked.

'A surfing one,' I whispered, holding it up for him to see.

'That magazine is a beauty,' Dad said and went back to the lounge room.

FACT — Not getting into trouble when your sister tries to get you busted is even better than getting her busted.

'Nyah, nyah, nyah, nyah, nyah,' I whispered to Jess, poking out my tongue. She flounced back to her room. I smiled to myself, picked up the magazine and went back to reading. Victory — how sweet it was!

As I read I heard the sound of a computer game in Jess's room. She was playing 'Need for Speed — Higher Stakes'. I smiled to myself. Jess was trying to beat me again. She tries to beat me at everything, but I've got the fastest time for all the different tracks of 'Need for Speed'.

FACT — Older sisters can't stand it if younger brothers beat them at something.

I didn't really care if she got a faster time than mine. I'd just have another go and beat her time again. It's funny, I don't really care about her beating me but when she starts turning something into a competition I just have to win. It's because she starts rubbing it in and gloating.

The funny thing is — although I'd never admit it out loud — even though Jess drives me berserk, I am the only one allowed to fight with her. If someone else starts picking on her they have to deal with me first.

Also, I have to admit, when Jess went off to camp this year, it was like she left a big hole in the house. I guess that means I missed her pestering me, but I'd never tell her that. She'd never let me live it down. I'd better make sure she doesn't get to read this. She'd give me a really hard time about it.

FACT — Even loathesome sisters are better then no sisters at all — you'd have no one to tease.

Anyway, on Saturday I read for a bit, then I went and raced Jess on the computer until it was time for the barbecue at our neighbour's place.

Painful Facts

FACT — When you get hurt parents always say, 'I told you so! Why do you have to learn the hard way?'

The hard way? What about the incredibly painful way? I know all about the painful facts of life.

Saturday night was a good example. We were having a barbecue next door for Mrs Giacobetti's fortieth birthday. There were lots of people from the street there and lots of her relatives. All the parents were standing around talking and all the kids were running around going mental. It was great, a sort of chasey game with no rules, just running and yelling. It was dark and I was flying along like a racing car in 'Need for Speed'.

FACT — You can run faster at night.

'Don't do that — you'll get hurt,' yelled Dad as I raced past.

Through the crowd, around the house, down the backyard, jump over the garden and BANG … There was an explosion in my head and then I was lying on the ground and my whole face felt like a peeled grape. My lips felt numb, one eye was blurry and when I touched the sore spot above my eye it was sticky and wet.

When I walked into the light of the pergola I heard my mother scream, 'Max! What have you done to yourself? What happened?'

Dad raced over and looked at my face. I hoped mine looked better than his. He was a kind of pale green colour, but I didn't think it was the right time to suggest *he* might need a doctor.

'That needs stitches,' he said. 'We'll have to take him to hospital.'

Dad raced off to get the car keys while Mum fussed over me like an old hen. (I didn't think it was the right time to say that either.) She wiped my face with a wet washer and then made me hold it like a pad over my cut eyebrow.

Dad came back waving the keys and they bundled me into the car. Jess wanted to come too, but she had to stay with Mrs Giacobetti. Ha! They were probably scared she'd faint from seeing the blood.

As we drove down the road Dad said, 'I told you someone would get hurt. *Why do you always have to learn the hard way?'*

Yeah, like I planned it!

Some Driving Facts

Dad was in racing mode. Mum was in back-seat-driver mode.

'Slow down!' she said. 'Indicate!' she ordered. 'Watch out!' she shouted, grabbing the dashboard and stamping hard on the floor.

'I am!' snapped Dad. 'Who's driving this thing, me or you?'

'Well, perhaps I should,' said Mum, very carefully.

'Look, the extra stress could be bad for your health,' Dad said and just put his foot down further.

'Mum's health? What about mine,' I thought.

Eighth Clue: I'm the one with the busted head, but Dad's worried about Mum's health.

As we neared the traffic lights even I started to get nervous. Dad hates red traffic lights. They were green and the nearer we got to them the faster he went. Then when we got really close they went orange.

Dad floored it and we crossed the lights just as they turned red.

FACT — Dads think orange lights mean 'go faster'.

Mum slumped back in her seat. There were finger marks pressed into the dash. I'm certain there was a right footprint pressed into the passenger side floor of the car. I think her scream was too high for human hearing, but I'm sure all the nearby dogs started barking.

Dad was pleased with himself.

Then we saw a flashing blue light beside the freeway up ahead. The freeway lit up like a Christmas tree with red brake lights. Dad tried to slow down without stamping on the brakes.

The police were booking someone in a four-wheel drive. The driver was nodding like a cocky in a cage with someone going, 'Dance cocky, dance cocky'.

The police weren't even looking in our direction, but Dad gripped the steering wheel and looked as guilty as our dog does when you catch him digging in the garden.

FACT — Drivers always look guilty when they see a police officer, even if they haven't done anything wrong.

FACT — Everyone slows down even if they weren't speeding.

Dad kept looking into the rear-vision mirror for ages afterwards.

Mum just said, 'Lucky it wasn't a multinova!'

As we drove along my cut was stinging, so I started looking at the other drivers to take my mind off it. I noticed a couple of facts about life on the freeway.

FACT — Drivers pick their noses on the freeway.

FACT — The other lane always moves faster than the one you're in — till you change into it.

By now Dad was driving like a maniac again. I know he wanted to get me to the hospital as fast as he could, but the truth is he speeds all the time.

It is truly amazing how being behind the wheel

of the car changes my dad from being a quiet, pleasant sort of person into a short- tempered speed demon.

Dad tapped his fingers on the top of the steering wheel, glared at other drivers, shook his head at them as if they were idiots and said things like, 'Oh come on! Typical! Move over fool!'

FACT — Cars change normal people into maniacs.

Finally we got to the hospital. Mum seemed to know how everything worked. She pointed Dad straight for the Emergency Set Down Area. It was a sort of wide loop road that went under an overhanging roof. There was a 'Casualty' sign above a door. One lane was for ambulances and one was for people like us.

'You take him in, Love,' Dad said to Mum. 'I'll park the car.'

'The visitors' car park is just over there,' Mum pointed.

Thinking back, I should have noticed how familiar Mum was with the hospital but she was rushing me so much I didn't have time.

Ninth Clue: Either Mum could read a zillion road signs in super-fast time, or she'd been here before.

Waiting Room Facts

The casualty room was full. It seemed funny to me that after the high-speed race to get there, when we finally got inside we had to sit for years before anyone came near us.

FACT — The only emergency you see in an Emergency Waiting Room is on the sign on the door.

As we sat there, I looked around the waiting room. There were sick and injured people everywhere.

I watched one person blow his nose into his hanky. After he finished he wiped his nose and then he sneaked a look to see what had come out of his head.

I looked around and saw several other people

with colds. I studied them intently and one by one they all did the same. Well sort of! Everyone had their own method.

One man blew his nose and had a good look at his hanky. He didn't care if anyone saw him. I called this the *'Open Book Method'*.

One lady had a small peek just before she put her tissue into her bag. Better manners I suppose but she still looked! This method I called the *'Manners Method'*.

The funniest one was a man who was trying to be really refined. Looking into his hanky was too uncouth for him. He did a delicate little puff into his hanky and then put it away, but I spotted how he looked down his nose just before he closed it. This method I named the *'Hanky Hypocrite'* method.

At this point I have to confess. I do it myself — look I mean. Well, at least I don't pick my nose and eat it like some kids I could name.

FACT — People look into their hankies after they blow their noses.

What do they expect to find? Maybe a bit of brains or something. I know some snot looks too colourful to be real. You look at it and think, 'Did that come out of my head? That snot's not snot, 's not snot at all!' But it usually is, that is, unless it's some food that nearly goes down the wrong way while you are eating and when you cough some of it shoots up the back of your nose. You know it's there but you can't blow it out for ages until it's really coated with snot. Then it fires out like a bullet into your hanky.

It makes you wonder how much of your head is hollow. When you've been bodysurfing and the waves have dumped you and you bend over later that day, a couple of litres of water pour out of your nose. Where does it all come from?

Possible fact:

There is a large hole inside your head, up behind your nose, where snot and sea water hang around for a bit before suddenly gushing out.

One man peeked into his tissue and must have seen something radically interesting. His eyes widened a little and he seemed a bit reluctant to put the hanky away. Secretly he probably would have liked to put the hanky under a microscope and study it carefully.

I was waiting to see what happened the next time he blew his nose when a nurse stopped and asked Mum how she was doing. Mum said she was fine. I thought I knew all my mum's friends but I didn't know her. 'Well, see you next week,' said the nurse cheerily.

I wondered about that for a second or two but my head had started stinging again and I was about to see a doctor so I didn't note it down straightaway.

Tenth Clue: Mum was being really chummy with mysterious nurses.

Next thing, a nurse was calling my name.

I gave the microscope man a look that said, 'I saw what you did!' and followed Dad and the nurse towards another room. Mum stayed put with a grotty waiting-room-type magazine.

FACT — Waiting-room magazines are always centuries old and boring, but adults always read them anyway.

Doctor Facts

The doctor's room was all stainless steel and white. It smelled antiseptic. The doctor was writing on a pad. He paid no attention to us so we stood there wondering what to do.

Finally, when we were feeling really embarrassed and uncomfortable he looked up.

'What can I do for you?' he asked Dad, as if I didn't exist. There I was standing with a blood-soaked cloth held to my face and he wanted to know what he could do for Dad.

'My son has a cut on his face,' said Dad. 'I think he needs stitches.'

'Do you?' replied the doctor, but his tone of voice said, 'How could you know? You're just a person. I'm the doctor around here!'

He came across to me. 'Now let's see what you've done to yourself,' he said and reached for the cloth.

Done to myself! It wasn't me! It was the stupid steel post in the garden.

The cloth was stuck to my head by dried blood.

'You should have used a wet washer,' he said accusingly.

'It was wet when we arrived!' said Dad.

But the doctor wasn't listening. He was talking to me.

'This might hurt a bit,' he said, wetting the cloth.

'Oh no!' I thought.

FACT — When doctors say something might hurt a bit, it is going to be screaming agony.

RIP!!!

'Aaargh!' I screamed. It felt like half my head was torn off. I looked across at Dad. 'Please rescue me, please, please!' my tortured eyes pleaded with him.

'Does this hurt?' asked the doctor.

'Oh no!' I thought.

'Aarrgh!' He squeezed the most tender, the most agony-filled part of my body — hard!

FACT — When doctors ask if something hurts, they are going to find the most painful part of your body and torture you with it.

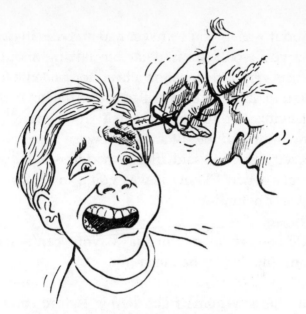

'Good, good, no nerve damage.'

'What a relief,' I said through gritted teeth. 'But keep going,' I thought, 'and you could still do some if you tried really hard.'

The doctor gave me a strange look and then went back to prodding my head.

'It does need stitches,' he admitted finally. He went across to a little table and picked up a syringe. 'This won't hurt at all,' he said.

'Oh no!'

FACT — When a doctor says something won't hurt at all it will probably be the worst pain ever.

And it was. If you've never had a needle in the head you won't know what I'm talking about. There is very little meat on a head for a needle to stick into. It felt like he drilled it into the bone — half-a-dozen times! Fortunately it eventually went numb and the stitching part wasn't too bad.

'Keep it dry,' he said after he had finished.

That's when I knew it was going to be forty degrees on Sunday.

FACT — If a doctor says you can't go swimming, it will be mega-hot.

On the way home I got the big lecture about how silly I had been and how I could have lost an eye. I knew they had to say it. It's their job. They have to look after you and stop you doing stupid things even if they are fun. So I said 'Yes Mum' and 'Yes Dad' every so often so they'd think I was listening.

Night-time Facts

Mum picked up Jess from next door. She came into my room to have a look at my cut. She was really impressed by the dressing. She thought it was excellent. I started to peel away some of the sticky stuff to show her the stitches but Dad said it was time to get some sleep.

I got into my pyjamas and lay in bed. Since the stitching, my head hadn't hurt at all, but now I was in bed it started aching. No matter how I tried to find a comfortable way to lie I couldn't. Have you ever noticed how pain is magnified at night? All day you hardly notice a sore spot but when it's time to go to sleep it hurts like mad.

FACT — Pain gets worse at night when you are trying to go to sleep.

I tossed and turned for hour after hour, lying this way, then that way, then this way again. I tried calling for Mum. 'Mum.' No answer. 'Muum!' No answer. Didn't they care?

'Muuumm!'

'What?' growled Dad's voice.

'My head hurts,' I said.

'Of course it hurts!' said Dad in an annoyed sounding voice. 'You're just going to have to try to ignore it and get some sleep.'

'Okay, Dad.' I said, trying to sound like a helpless but brave boy, but I got no reaction so I tried to get to sleep. I still couldn't sleep so I thought I would try counting sheep.

FACT — Counting sheep doesn't make you go to sleep.

First of all there are no sheep there so you have to imagine them. Secondly it takes so much effort to imagine even one sheep that you are more awake than you would have been if you just lay there. And if you do manage to imagine one, when you count it you have to start imagining another one.

The last thing I remember was lying there listening for monsters.

I woke up in pitch-blackness. My pillow was

gone and my sheets were all tangled. I tried to undo them in the dark but they had pulled out of the bottom of the bed. They were wound up into a ball that I couldn't get under. There I was lying on top of my bed in the pitch-black night with no sheets I could use to protect me from monsters. I untangled a little corner of the sheets and tried to get underneath but it didn't work. I had no choice. I had to get up and turn on the light.

One, two, three — I leapt off the bed towards the light switch.

Bang!

I bounced off something flat and hard that shouldn't have been there. My cut started throbbing. I reached out in the darkness to feel what I'd hit. It was a wall where a wall shouldn't have been. I felt my way down the wall to the bottom of my bed. Another wall!

There is no wall at the bottom of my bed! Where was I? What was going on? Everything was wrong. Nothing was where it was supposed to be. It was like being in a horror movie where the victim wakes up in the dungeon of a castle.

Finally I found the door and flipped on the light switch. The room looked just the same as always. I looked at my bed and there were my sheets, in a ball at the bottom, where my feet go. I must have been upside down.

FACT — Waking up in the pitch-black the wrong way up is even scarier than monsters.

So I made my bed, flipped off the light, leapt into bed and hauled the sheets over my head and lay there listening for monsters. All I could hear was my own breathing. And then I realised I was busting.

'Oh no!' I thought.

'One, two, three,' I jumped out of bed and headed for the light switch, but before I could get there, the light came on. There I was, frozen with shock, halfway across the room with my dad glaring at me from the doorway.

'What do you think you're doing?' he growled at me. His red eyes were fixed on my face like truth searchlights.

'I'm going to the toilet,' I said.

'You've been making enough noise to wake the dead for the last half an hour,' accused Dad.

Half an hour! No way was it half an hour! More like five minutes!

FACT — Parents always exaggerate how long you have been doing something they don't like.

'No way …' I began, but then I saw Dad's glaring red eyes. 'Sorry, Dad,' I grovelled, suddenly realising that I was very close to major disaster.

FACT — Sometimes nothing you say will help and it is better to shut up.

'Yes, well, hurry up and get straight back into bed! And I don't want to hear another peep out of you!' he growled.

I was down to the toilet and back in bed in Olympic-record time.

I lay awake for a while wondering why Dad had got up instead of Mum. It's always Mum who comes in the night. She says Dad could sleep through a bomb. But he'd got up last night as well.

Eleventh Clue: Dad wasn't sleeping too well.

Sunday Morning Facts

I must have dropped off because the next thing I knew it was morning. I knew it was too early to get up because the sun was just coming up. My face was hurting but I felt good otherwise. I thought about lying in bed until Mum and Dad got up. I could try to get breakfast in bed seeing as how I was terribly injured. But when I thought some more I realised that if I did get breakfast in bed I would have to hang around all day acting like an invalid. It would have been a total waste of a Sunday so I decided to get dressed and sneak outside to play.

FACT — Being sick is only worth it on school days.

FACT — If you convince your parents that you

are nearly dying in the morning you can't miraculously recover later on or parents will get really mad.

As I flung the covers off, the sheets flicked across my face and hurt the stitches. I sat down for a second until they stopped hurting and then I took off my pyjama shirt, grabbed my favourite T-shirt from the floor and put it on. As I pulled it over my head the tight neck dragged across the stitches and hurt them again.

FACT — If you have a sore part on your body everything in the world wants to bump it or scrape it.

I finished dressing and tiptoed out of my room. I was starving so I snuck into the kitchen to get a before-breakfast snack.

I opened the fridge, got out some milk and gently put the carton on the table. Next I opened the pantry and carried the muesli to the table. I tiptoed back to the cupboards for a plate and spoon and took them to the table. So far, so good.

There was only the slightest little rustle as I poured the muesli into the bowl and a tiny splashing sound as I poured the milk over it. I did it all without making any sound loud enough for human ears to hear, especially from the other end of the house. I gently dipped the spoon into the cereal and lifted a spoonful into my mouth. Crunch, crunch. I began to chew it with my mouth closed.

'Stop making all that racket!' roared Dad at the top of his voice. 'You'll wake Mum!'

I tried chewing quietly.

FACT — It is impossible to chew quietly if someone is listening.

I could hear every chew like a rock being crushed inside my head. Then I tried to swallow. It sounded like a dunny flushing.

FACT — It is impossible to swallow quietly if someone is listening.

I could almost feel Dad listening from his room. I could sense him putting his head under the pillow trying to muffle the sound of my chewing. I could almost see him waiting for the next chewing or swallowing noise.

I couldn't stand it, so I took my bowl and went outside onto the back lawn to eat the rest of it.

It was a beautiful morning and my breakfast tasted much better out there anyway.

Climbing Facts

As I ate I looked around the yard and I noticed my model aeroplane up in the tree. It got stuck up in the top branches last night when we were at the next-door neighbours barbeque. I knew I shouldn't have flown it in the dark but the other kids kept on and on at me until I did. It got stuck the first throw I did. Straight over the fence and into our tree, like a homing pigeon. It was too dark to get it down so I left it up there.

Somehow in the morning it didn't look that high up. I thought I could climb up close enough to grab it.

I had a bit of trouble getting started because the bottom branches were a bit high for me to reach, and our dog kept leaping around me like it had gone berko. I got a chair and stood on it, and I managed to get hold of the lowest branch.

I tried to pull myself straight up onto the branch but my arms weren't strong enough. I tried getting a foothold by sticking my toes into little splits in the bark but that didn't work either, so then I tried swinging my legs up and wrapping them around the branch. With a little struggling and wrestling I finally managed to get up.

FACT — The bottom branch of a tree is usually the hardest to climb onto.

I looked down. I was pretty high up already and I had only just begun. I looked up and there were lots of branches to hang onto so I figured it would be easy, but as I climbed closer to the plane the branches got thinner and thinner.

Then I looked down again. I shouldn't have! I was even higher than the roof of our house. I could see into the backyards of all our neighbours. I could see all of our backyard from above and it looked pretty small down there. I was up in the tree, higher than I had ever been outside a skyscraper, and the model aeroplane was still about two metres out of reach on the end of a long branch.

FACT — A tree is higher looking down from the top than it is looking up from the bottom.

Three questions filled my mind. How could I get the aeroplane down? How could I get myself down? Would I live?

In movies, people always tell someone in a dangerous high place, 'Don't look down!' This is all very well but when you are in a tree how can you climb down if you can't look where to put your feet? Anyway, my aeroplane was still there.

It was just sort of resting in the fork of a branch, so I gave the branch a shake. My own branch started swaying. I grabbed hold of the tree with both hands and hung on for dear life. The stupid aeroplane could stay there for all I cared. I would rather stay alive.

It took me ages to climb down but in the end I reached the lowest branch. The only way I could get down was to hang by my arms and let myself drop to the ground. I lay there and thought of one more fact about climbing.

FACT — It is easier climbing up than it is climbing down.

I recovered for a while and then I looked up at my aeroplane. It was too high for me to use a rake to knock it down. I needed some other plan. Then I had a brainwave. Throw something up to knock it down! The trouble was I had forgotten a very important fact.

FACT — Tree branches keep more than they give back.

I started with my footy, but that stuck up there too. Then I thought I'd try something heavier, like a cricket ball, but somehow that got stuck in the branches too.

So I got the rake. I was swinging it and throwing it up like a big, whirly helicopter blade but the aeroplane stayed put. I was just getting cheesed off when one last throw made it drop down several branches, so I could now reach the branch it was on with the rake. I was jumping up and down, pushing the branch to make it shake, when the cricket ball came down and nearly knocked me out. It only just missed my head and hit me on my shoulder. I figured that shaking the tree from underneath wasn't a good idea so I went back and had one more throw with the rake. It stuck fast above the aeroplane.

Then Dad came out of the house. He'd been watching me and he thought it was time to show me how it was done.

FACT — If kids are having trouble doing something, parents always have to take over.

He took off one of his joggers and let fly, scoring a direct hit on my model aeroplane. It came down, but his shoe stayed up there. He looked at me but I didn't smile even though I was cracking up inside. When he went off to get something I did a little victory routine on the lawn. Not so clever now, are you Dad!

He came back with a brick. It was so heavy that it always came down. After a while, so did the football and the rake and his shoe. Unfortunately, the brick landed right in the middle of one of Mum's plants on the last throw. Dad and I straightened the leaves out and stood the flower up before we went in for breakfast. By then I was hungry again.

As we walked towards the house I saw Jess looking out of her bedroom window. I was certain she'd tell on us, but she didn't. Amazing!

My Room Facts

At breakfast Mum was on the warpath. I think she was feeling sick again. It seemed like she was sick every morning lately.

'Don't use all the milk!' she snapped at me. 'Think about the rest of us.'

'There're two litres in the fridge,' I pointed out.

'That's beside the point,' Mum said. 'You always use too much milk and there is never enough for the rest of us.'

'Jess used just as much,' I said.

'I did not!' snapped Jess.

'You did!' I repeated.

'I did not!'

'You did!'

'You didn't!'

'I did!' I yelled.

Jess just sat there grinning at me until I realised she'd got me again.

'That's enough,' growled Mum. 'Anyway, two wrongs don't make a right.'

'But there're two litres left in the fridge,' I argued, but at that point she got on to my room.

MY room! That's a laugh!

FACT — Your room is not really yours at all.

My room is supposed to be MY ROOM. Mum and Dad call it YOUR ROOM. What I want to know is why my mum always has to tell me where the furniture has to go? It's my room until I try to move my bed and all the rest of my stuff around. Then Mum comes in with fifty million reasons why the way I want it is no good and why I have to have it how she wants me to have it.

It's not only the bed and stuff; it's all my junk. Mum wants it put away, tidily.

FACT — A person's room is really comfortable when it's a bit messy. Not too messy, just a bit.

FACT — Your mum can't stand it if your room is comfortably messy.

After breakfast Mum sent me into my room to

tidy it up. I sat on the bed to think about where to start and where I would put everything this time.

As I was thinking about where to put things I noticed a comic on the floor. It was an old one that I had read lots of times before but for some reason it was much more interesting than cleaning up my room.

'I'll just have a quick look at it,' I thought to myself.

I was lying on my bed reading it when Mum came into the room. She nearly went into orbit.

'What do you think you are doing?' she bellowed.

'Cleaning up my room?' I answered, hopefully. I might as well have worn red undies in a bullpen. I was busted.

First she looked at my clothes, screwed up on the floor in the corner.

FACT — Your dirty clothes are supposed to be in the laundry but they're usually scrunched up on the floor.

'I did the washing yesterday. Why weren't your dirty clothes in the laundry basket?' she yelled. She was getting red in the face. It was a bad sign.

'Get them out there — NOW!' she ordered, 'Or you're grounded for a week.'

I thought this was a bit strong but realised that it wasn't quite the time to say so. I grabbed the pile of clothes and was just shoving it in the laundry when I found my favourite pair of shorts in the middle of the bundle. These shorts were like my best friends. True, they were getting a few holes in them and they had faded so much it was hard to see the pattern on them anymore, but they were really comfortable and I thought they were cool.

FACT — Mums don't like your favourite faded old shorts with holes in them.

FACT — Favourite old shorts never return from the wash.

I carefully screwed them up and stashed them in the back of my wardrobe. I was just about to relax with the comic again when Mum came into the room. I waited to see what she'd pick on now.

She looked at my study desk. 'How on earth do you expect to be able to study with all that mess on there?' she asked.

I don't know about you, but I figure that you don't do your homework on your study desk.

FACT — Study desks are where you put all your junk that you don't put on the floor.

FACT — You don't do your homework at your study desk, you do it in the dining room where you are in everyone's way.

Anyway Mum made me tidy up the desk and put everything away — not where I wanted to put it in MY ROOM, but where Mum said MY stuff should be in MY ROOM. I felt like starting a kids' revolution but if I did Dad would just say I was already revolting. Ha. Ha. Some days I can't win.

FACT — Some days you are going to get into trouble no matter what.

Bathroom Facts

By the time I'd finished it was time to get ready to visit Grandma and Grandpa, so thankfully I could escape into the shower before Mum could find anything else to go ballistic about. I wore Mum's shower cap to protect my stitches. It's got flowers all over it so I was glad no one could see me. I had the water turned up full bore, as hot as I could bear it, and started singing my head off.

FACT — You sound like a rock star in the shower.

FACT — No one else agrees.

Bang, Bang. 'Cut out that racket! You sound like you've got a stomach-ache,' Dad yelled.

He can talk. His Elvis imitations are total noise
pollution.

Perhaps it was just the song he didn't like, so I
decided to change it and launched into a
dynamic version of:

> *In the jungle,*
> *The mighty jungle,*
> *The lion sleeps tonight.*
> *In the jungle …*

BANG, BANG, BANG.

'Cut it out!' yelled Dad a little louder than before.

> *A wim a way*
> *A wim a way …*

'Shardup!' yelled Dad in his 'You've gone too far' voice.

FACT — Parents have a *'Don't push your luck any further'* voice.

FACT — You always push your luck until you hear that voice.

FACT — Sometimes you push just a bit further.

'Okay, Dad,' I said, 'you just had to ask. Perhaps if I did one of your favourite songs, hey?'

I could feel him radiating anger through the bathroom door like laser beams, so I started making loud shower noises instead.

As soon as I finished soaping up my face I dropped the soap. Keeping my eyes tight shut, I felt around on the bottom of the shower, but I couldn't find it so I had to take a peek. Big mistake!

FACT — Soap always gets into your eyes.

I turned my face straight towards the nozzle. I hoped like mad that no one else in the house turned on a tap right at this moment.

FACT — If someone uses a tap in the house while you're having a shower, it will go either freezing cold or boiling hot.

FACT — Your face is the last place you want the water squirting on when it goes freezing cold or boiling hot. (Or *nearly* the last place.)

Right then, as I was facing the nozzle, the water went sub-zero. I yelled and tried to jump out from under the water, but I jumped the wrong way and I ended up trying to flatten myself against the wall. Some freezing water was still spraying on me so I squashed up into the corner and reached down the wall under the shower and grabbed the cold tap. I turned it down and the shower became a weak little dribble, but at least it was warm so I stepped back under it.

Right then the pressure came back and the water went boiling hot. This time I jumped the other way, right out through the shower curtain.

Water sprayed all over the bathroom floor.

I figured that enough was enough. For the first time in ages I had finished my shower before Mum or Dad banged on the door and told me to stop before I used up all the hot water.

FACT — Parents can have showers for as long as they want but kids can't.

As I reached for a towel I caught sight of myself in the mirror. It was too much to resist. Hey, when you've got it flaunt it, that's my motto. I did lots of poses in front of the mirror, in the nude. Frontwards, sideways, stomach in, stomach out, chest in, chest out. Hair slicked back. Hair falling forward over one eye.

FACT — You have to pose in front of the mirror after a shower.

But, all good things have to end — Dad wanted to have his shower.

FACT — After you have a shower, parents will always say that you've flooded the bathroom.

Sure enough Dad made me get a towel and mop up all the water. I must remember to have my shower before Jess, then she'll have to dry the floor.

I stood on the towels and did skiddies around the bathroom to dry the floor and then I went and got dressed.

I heard the toilet flush and then Mum came in singing, 'A wim a way, A wim a way ...'

FACT — Some songs get stuck in your head and you just can't stop singing them.

FACT — They are usually songs you can't stand.

Sunday Drive Facts

We were finally ready and went out to the car. All except Dad. We waited in the car but he didn't come so Mum went to look for him. He was in the toilet — reading.

FACT — Whenever you have to go somewhere your parents hassle you to get ready but you always wind up waiting for one of them.

Grandma's house is way out in the hills and before long I realised that I was feeling thirsty.

'Mum, I need a drink.'

'Why didn't you have one before we left?' she snapped, rolling her eyes upwards towards the sky.

'I wasn't thirsty then,' I explained.

Dad exploded. 'You always do this,' he yelled,

'Every time we go anywhere.'

FACT — Kids get thirsty about ten minutes after setting out on a long drive.

'No I don't ...' I started to argue, but then I realised it was like I was doing a full on, bottom wiggling lambada, in red undies, in a pen full of angry bulls.

'You'll just have to wait until we see a petrol station,' Dad said in his 'Don't-push-your-luck' voice.

After what must have been hours I thought I'd better remind Mum that I was still thirsty, in case she had forgotten.

'Mum, I'm still really thirsty,' I whined in my most pathetically thirsty voice.

They both exploded at me for nagging. Mum was yelling something about it only being five minutes since the last time I asked. Why parents have to exaggerate I don't know.

FACT — Time goes slower for kids than for parents on car trips.

I sat in the back for a couple more centuries. Mum started humming, 'In the jungle, the mighty jungle ...'

Twelfth Clue: Sudden changes of mood; one minute she's yelling and the next she's singing.

Just as I was about to expire from a mouth so dry that my raspy tongue was sticking to my cracked, parched lips, we pulled into a service station.

Mum raced off to the toilet while Dad put petrol in the car.

He was patting himself on the back for having found petrol two cents a litre cheaper than the service station near home, and he filled the petrol tank to the brim. He shook the nozzle of the petrol pump so that it rattled before he took it out and put it back on the pump. He always does that.

I looked around the service station as Dad was paying, and I noticed that all the men shook the nozzle when they finished. The women just took the nozzle straight out.

FACT — Men shake anything that looks like a hose when they have finished squirting it.

Dad came out of the shop with a large bottle of cool drink. We had to share. I hate sharing!

FACT — Everyone else gets more than you do when you have to share.

When it was my turn I poured cool drink down my throat like the Solo Man, but it fizzed up and some went up the back of my nose. I coughed and some spurted out of my nose. It really stung and my eyes watered. Mum was not impressed.

'Don't drink it all!' Mum complained. 'Think about the rest of us.'

Jess tried to drink as much as me, but it fizzed up on her too and she had a major coughing fit. I helped by patting her back, extra hard, so she wouldn't choke. And she didn't even thank me.

Down the highway a few hundred metres we

passed another service station with cheaper fuel for sale. Dad was upset. He hates it when something like that happens. If he could, he'd return the petrol he'd just bought.

FACT — Parents can be quite happy about the price they pay for anything until they see it for less somewhere else — then they feel ripped off.

Peeing In The Bush Facts

A little further down the road I realised that I needed to go to the toilet.

FACT — When you have a drink in a car it makes you want to go to the toilet almost straightaway.

FACT — Don't tell your parents that you need to go to the toilet just after you leave a petrol station or they go ballistic.

'Mum, I need to have a pee,' I said.

Both Mum and Dad groaned out loud.

Dad said, 'I don't believe it! We just left a service station with a perfectly good toilet. Why on earth didn't you go there?'

'I didn't need to go then,' I said.

'Well, you'll just have to go behind a tree.'

I didn't care one bit. There is something very fine about peeing in the bush. A certain sense of freedom you just don't get in the toilet. I like how you don't have to be so careful about where you aim. Which is funny because there are more interesting things to aim at, so you end up aiming more carefully than ever. There is a lot of satisfaction in nearly drowning an ant or making a pattern in the sand or wetting a whole patch on the side of the tree. I personally have once written my name in running writing on the ground.

While Dad looked for a nice patch of bush I started to sing.

> *Driving down the highway,*
> *Doing ninety-eight,*
> *Looking for a toilet,*
> *Bwart — too late!*

Mum and Dad didn't seem to see the funny side, so after singing it a few times I started looking for a nice patch of bush as well.

'What about that one?' I asked.

'Not enough trees,' said Dad. 'People will be able to see you from the road.'

'What about that one then?' I said, pointing at a patch of trees further down the road.

'I don't want to stop on a blind bend,' Dad said.

'What's a blind bend, Dad?' I asked.

'It's a bend in the road that you can't see around,' he told me.

'Why don't you want to stop on a blind bend?' I asked.

'So a car won't crash into us,' said Dad, a little impatiently.

'Why would a car crash into us?' I asked innocently.

'Because the driver wouldn't see us until it was too late,' Dad growled.

'Why?' I asked.

'Because!' snapped Dad.

'Because why?' I asked.

Dad had had enough. He grunted something and pulled over. 'Just go to the toilet,' he said wearily.

FACT — Sometimes parents give up quicker if you ask millions of questions.

I climbed out of the car and ran for the trees, straight onto some prickles, in my bare feet.

FACT — You never tread on a prickle until you are in the middle of a huge patch of them.

FACT — After you tread on one prickle, every step you take is on another prickle.

FACT — When you sit down to pull a prickle out of your foot you sit on the worst prickle of all.

I was in big trouble. There was no point turning back so I just kept heading for the tree, where I planned to pee. Ow! Ow! Ow! Ow! — until I was out of the prickles and on soft grass. I carefully picked a spot to sit down so I could pull the prickles out of my feet. OWW! A big prickle stuck right into the bony part of my bum.

Typical!

I finally found a safe patch and pulled out all the prickles I could get hold of. Some of them had snapped off in my feet and I knew I would have to ask Mum to pull them out with tweezers, or dig them out with a needle.

I also knew what Dad was going to say ... 'Why do you always have to learn the hard way?'

FACT — Knowing what your parents are going to say only makes it worse.

Anyway, I pulled out all the prickles I could and stood up to have my pee. Just as I started I saw an ant trail about five steps away. I really wanted to flood the middle of the trail so the ants would get lost and scatter and wander around in circles. There was one big problem. I had already started to pee.

FACT — Once you start peeing you can't stop.

I waddled across to the ant trail, still peeing, but just as I got there I ran out. Empty! Was I disappointed! I had used up all my flooding time waddling along, like one of those impact sprinklers they use to water ovals.

I kicked some dirt into the middle of the ant trail and the ants scattered everywhere. I watched them for a while and then the bushes next to me rustled loudly. I nearly had a heart attack! I was sure it was a snake, but when I looked it was just a lizard looking back at me from under the bushes.

FACT — When a bush rustles next to you, you always think it's a snake or something else really dangerous.

I was really relieved but my heart was still beating like Tarzan beats his chest after he has wrestled a rubber crocodile.

By this time Dad was getting impatient and beeping the horn so I hurried back to the car.

'What were you doing sitting under the tree?' Mum asked.

I told her I was pulling prickles out of my feet.

'Where are your shoes?' Dad asked.

'On the floor of the car,' I told him.

'What good are they to you there? You should have had them on. I told you to put them on before we left. Why didn't you?' Dad nagged.

'My feet would have been too hot,' I argued.

'But you wouldn't have prickles in them. Why do you always have to learn the hard way?'

He said it! I was ready for it but it still annoyed me half to death. I sat there for a while plotting revenge but then I started to get bored.

'Are we nearly there yet?' I asked.

'Soon,' said Dad.

I waited ages. I tried looking out at the passing scenery. I tried to get Mum and Dad to play 'I Spy' but they wouldn't. Jess was no fun at all so I started to imitate her.

'Stop it,' she said.

'Stop it,' I repeated.

'Mum, Factso is copying me.'

'Mum, Factso is …'

'Cut it out!' yelled Dad. 'If we have a crash it'll be your fault.'

'Yeah, right! Like I'm driving,' I thought, but I didn't say anything.

We drove on for a while and then I asked, 'Are we nearly there yet?'

'Soon!' snapped Dad. 'Don't ask again. It's only five minutes since you asked last time.'

Ages later when I was bored mindless, I asked, 'Are we nearly there yet?' one more time.

You'd think I was a mega-criminal or something. Dad told me that if I asked once more I'd have to get out and walk, but just then we reached Grandma and Grandpa's.

Grandparent Facts

I love my grandma and grandpa. No matter what I do, they think I'm great. It's a pity the drive to their house is so long and Mum makes us wear daggy clothes when we go.

FACT — Grandparents think you're great no matter what you do.

As we pulled up in the driveway we saw Grandma digging near her rose bushes. She spends heaps of time in her garden. She grows lots of different plants, but her favourites are her roses. I hate roses.

FACT — If there are rose bushes in the garden, sooner or later, they'll get you.

I decided to stay right away from them. I thought about how I could get up the path without one of them reaching out and ripping my clothes or scratching me across the leg. I figured I would stick to the exact dead centre of the path.

By the time I had worked out my plan of action Grandpa was coming out of his shed and Grandma was at the car door. She hugged and kissed Mum and Dad like she hadn't seen them for years instead of just a week. Dad and Mum stood there smiling like they had done something really clever. Dad hugged Mum and rubbed her tummy instead of patting her on the bottom like he usually does.

This seemed to mean something, but what? I glanced at Jess and she gave me one of those 'I know something you don't' looks again.

Thirteenth Clue: Mum and Dad were being really smug and it seemed to have something to do with Mum's stomach!?

Then Grandma turned to Jess and me. I knew what was about to happen.

FACT — Grandparents always pinch your cheek and say how much you've grown, and then slobber all over you.

She gave us each a big hug and a giant sloppy kiss on the cheek. SMACK! My face was soaked. Then she pinched my cheek. 'Look how you've grown. You're becoming a handsome young man.'

'I used to be before my face was stretched out of shape,' I thought.

Then, as usual, Grandma pushed my hair over to one side, nerd style, and saw the stitches above my eye.

'What happened to your face?' she gasped.

'He head-butted a steel garden post on Friday night,' said Dad.

Grandpa smiled at Dad, but Grandma took no notice of him. She started fussing over me and shooing me towards the house for some lemonade and biscuits. Unfortunately, she shooed me to one side of the path. You guessed it, a rose bush snagged my shirt and dragged me close enough for a thorn to scratch me.

Grandma began to fuss even more. I made the most of it and told her about the prickles in my feet. But not too loud, I didn't want to start Mum and Dad up again. Grandma put some ointment on the scratch and then gave me the lemonade and biscuits.

FACT — Grandmother lemonade and biscuits are the best.

I bit my biscuit and crumbled it in my mouth. Then I had a sip of lemonade. It was really fizzy and little bubbles hit me in the face as I sipped it. I mixed the lemonade with the biscuit crumbs in my mouth and made a sort of thick, sweet, gluey paste. It was hard to swallow so I had another sip of lemonade and the whole lot fizzed up in my mouth. My cheeks were bulging out and some nearly came out of my ears before I managed to swallow. It was good fun so I did it again. Then I noticed that everyone except Grandma was watching me.

'Ahh, grosso Factso,' Jess said in her usual whiney voice.

I acted like nothing was happening.

When we finished eating and Grandma finished fussing over my mortal wounds, everyone stood around in the kitchen talking.

Grandma and Mum got busy making lunch. Dad stood with his back to the stove talking to Grandpa. He looked like he was warming his bottom but it was the middle of summer.

FACT — People stand around stoves and heaters warming their bottoms even when they're not turned on.

I got sick of standing around, and the biscuits and lemonade had run out, so I went for a wander through the house. Have you ever noticed how quiet grandparents' houses are? As I walked down the hall towards the back I could hear all the noise from the kitchen but back here it was really silent and old smelling.

I went down the steps into the backyard. Grandpa and Grandma's backyard is great. They have loads of strange plants all over the place.

There are tons of them in pots. Grandpa's cactus plants, if you can call them plants, come in the weirdest shapes and sizes and colours. Some are really, really small and some are huge with giant spines. I've learnt not to touch any of them. The giant spines look really wicked and painful, but the small hairy ones are the worst. If you touch one of them you get millions and millions of tiny spines in your skin and you can't pull them out. You just have to wait for them to come out by themselves.

FACT — You should leave cacti completely alone. But even when you do, somehow they can still jump at you when you're not watching.

I made my way down the path to Grandpa's shed. The door was open so I went in to look at what cool stuff he had this time.

FACT — Grandpas have great stuff in their sheds.

I thought about making a Jess trap, but before I could get started I heard Mum calling me in for lunch.

Table Manners Facts

Here are some facts about Sunday lunches at grandparents' houses.

FACT — The vegetables will be cooked until they're mushy.

FACT — You have to eat with knives and forks.

FACT — Forks will not pick up peas.

Anyway we all sat around and ate lunch and every fact happened: the vegetables were mushy, we had to eat with knives and forks, and I couldn't pick up the peas. Then, when I was trying to cut my meat the stupid fork slipped and peas went all over the floor.

Mum was really embarrassed. She tried to give

me some of hers. I thought this was fair enough because Grandma had piled Mum's plate up with much more food than she usually eats, but Grandma wouldn't hear of it.

'You need it,' she said to Mum, 'especially now.'

I did think it was strange at the time. If Grandma knew how many diet books Mum had at home she'd really freak out. Mum would never eat that much at home.

Fourteenth Clue: Grandma was trying to fatten Mum up.

I was just going to ask Grandma about this when I had an accident. A piece of potato, covered in gravy, slipped off my fork and made a gravy trail down my shirt.

I was in disgrace. I had been trying to get the last bit of food into my mouth using the fork. It would have been easier if I could have used the fork in my right hand. It was in my left hand, with my knife in the right, because it's supposed to be good manners. How can you have good manners when you're chasing the last bit of food round and round the plate?

Then I saw Grandpa wink at me. He smiled and pushed his false teeth out of his mouth and

made them do chomps in the air. It was really cool and I was grinning about it when Grandma said, 'Joe, that's disgusting! You're supposed to be setting a good example!'

'Yes, Dear,' said Grandpa, but I could tell he didn't mean it. He gave me another secret wink. Grandpa is cool.

After lunch Mum said Jess and I would do the dishes. Luckily for us Grandma wouldn't hear of it. 'Off you go and play,' she said, 'children need to be out in the fresh air.' We shot through before Mum could say anything.

We mucked around the backyard for a bit and then we heard Grandpa and Dad yelling.

They were watching footy on TV.

Footy On Telly Facts

Jess and I sat on the couch between Dad and Grandpa.

There we were, in the lounge room, yelling abuse at the other team and the umpire, cheering when our team did something good and ignoring it when our team got away with some dirty play. After all, the other team were such dirty players that it was only evening things up a little.

FACT — Everyone yells at the umpire, even if they're on the telly and can't hear you.

FACT — Umpires always favour the other team.

FACT — The other team cheats.

The more we yelled and carried on the more fun it was and the more annoyed Mum and Grandma got. They started to think of jobs Dad and Grandpa should do — jobs that needed to be finished yesterday. But they wouldn't budge.

Dad patted the couch next to him. 'Sit down, Dear, you need to put your feet up and have a rest,' he said to Mum.

Mum snorted, 'You call that rest? Yelling at the telly?' She turned and went to sit in the backyard with Grandma. She just doesn't know what real fun is.

FACT — Some people just can't stand it when other people are having fun watching footy.

Every time some adverts came on Dad and Grandpa would send Jess or me for some potato chips or beer or something else to eat.

FACT — Adults make kids slaves when footy is on.

After a while the other team started to win. Dad and Grandpa got madder and madder. I thought Dad was about to rip his cushion to pieces when Grandpa suggested that they go and do something else. They wandered around the backyard and house not really doing anything, and about every five minutes they turned the telly on to check the score.

After a while our team started to catch up and when they got really close we sat down again to watch it. The nearer the game got to the end and the closer the scores got, the louder we all yelled and the redder Grandpa's and Dad's faces went.

'Aargh!' yelled Dad. 'What about that, umpire?'

'You've got to be joking!' yelled Grandpa.

'About time!' shouted Dad.

Dead silence.

'Come on, come on,' they both muttered. 'Yeehaa! Wahoo!' they both screamed in ecstasy.

FACT — The louder you yell, the more fun it is.

When our team finally won at the last second, Dad and Grandpa did a war dance, which is strange, because Mum says Dad wouldn't even dance at their wedding. Afterwards Grandpa was in a generous mood.

'How would you like to make some pocket money washing my car?' he asked.

'Unreal!' I thought. 'Grandpa pays heaps.'

Car Washing Facts

We washed the car on the front lawn. We had to hose it down and then scrub it with a foamy sponge. I got the hose first.

FACT — When you have the hose you have to squirt someone.

FACT — You can only pretend it was an accident once.

I squirted the car over first and Jess rubbed the dirt off with the sponge. She had a bucket with water and detergent in it. When she finished one bit and moved on to the next bit, I had to squirt off all the soapsuds.

Jess was crouching down scrubbing the front bumper and completely by accident, without any planning at all, I squirted across the bonnet and got her on the head. Freezing water ran down her neck and wet her shirt. She screamed, jumped up and wiped her face with her hands, which were covered with soapsuds. Some got in her eyes and she yelled even louder.

'Sorry,' I said. For some unknown reason she didn't believe me and yelled even louder.

'What's going on?' Dad shouted from the door.

Of course my rotten, dobber sister had to tell Dad that I did it on purpose and he busted me and she got the hose. I had to do the scrubbing while she got to squirt all the suds off.

'You're dead meat, Jess!' I whispered.

'What was that?' growled Dad, looking at me.

'What?' I said. 'How come you're picking on me?'

Dad just glared at me and went inside and Jess and I started on the back of the car.

Jess was glaring at me. She was planning revenge so I told her she couldn't squirt me because she might wet my stitches.

I started scrubbing the bonnet and I had to lean right over it to get the dirt off near the windscreen. Big mistake! When I stood up my T-shirt was wet and it slapped back and stuck all over my stomach.

FACT — Your stomach is the worst place to get slapped by a cold, wet T-shirt.

I leaned forwards, sucking in my stomach, and walked away from the car. Oooh! Ooooh! Oooh! I pulled the T-shirt over my head and it slopped onto the ground.

I figured I'd better wring the water out of it so it would dry faster. I grabbed it by the ends and started to twist. It wound up into a rope and then it started to curl up into knots. The tighter I twisted, the more water came out of it. Then I opened it out, but it had changed shape. It was much shorter and much wider than before and it had baggy bits hanging out of places where it used to be straight.

'You've wrecked it,' said Jess. 'It's stuffed! You're going to be so busted!'

'It'll go back into shape when it's dry,' I told her, kind of hopefully, and hung it up over the garden gate.

We went back to washing the car and before we had finished Jess had managed to squirt me in the legs twice (by accident — she reckoned) and in the back once. The difference between us is I didn't go squealing to Dad first chance I got.

Instead I waited until she turned the hose off and stepped away from it, then I grabbed it and turned it on full bore and squirted her all over. She tried to get away but I had her cornered by the house. She was squealing and shouting but I just kept squirting her until I had had enough revenge.

Then I started squirting the water straight up in the air and making falling water patterns. There was a big splattering where the water hit the ground. The splattering raced all over the lawn, depending on where I pointed the hose.

I tried to get the water to chase Jess when she came back but she ran around the side of the house again. Weak!

I had fun trying to get the splatters to come as close to me as I could without them actually getting me. It was exciting because the water was freezing and was splattering red mud up out of the grass. I got a bit wet a couple of times when it charged straight at me and went behind and then came back past me, but I was getting pretty good at controlling it.

I was just planning to chase Jess all around the yard with it when she charged out from the side of the house with a bucket of water. I was looking up so I didn't know she was there until it hit me. One second I was nearly dry, the next I was soaked. And freezing!

I was chasing her when Mum and Dad came out of the house to see how the car washing was going. We got busted s-o-o-o badly! Jess got extra busted for wetting my stitches. I stood behind Mum and Dad and made faces at her when they weren't looking.

And then Mum asked me what I had done with my shirt so I told her it was drying out and I went to get it off the gate. It was still the same wide, short shape, and when I picked it up I knew I was going to be grounded for life. The gate had put a crisscross rusty pattern all over the back. It was too late to try anything. All I could do was walk back and show her.

She went ballistic and Dad went ballistic too. I reminded them that Jess wet it but they weren't listening. They were telling me off and apologising to Grandma and Grandpa for our behaviour at the same time. I mostly looked at the ground but every so often I snuck a look at Grandma and Grandpa. I never planned to upset them.

One time when I looked at Grandpa he caught my eye and winked. Yes, no matter what you do, they think you're great. It's a fact! I love them!

End Of The Weekend Facts

Jess and I slept all the way home. It was great. I didn't have to sit there getting bored for the whole drive.

FACT — The best way to cope with a long drive is to sleep through the whole thing.

The trouble was, when we got home, Jess and I were wide-awake and Mum and Dad were exhausted. They wanted us to go to bed straightaway. We tried all the excuses and everything.

'No way!' said Dad. 'It's a school day tomorrow. By the way, have you finished your homework?'

'Yes,' said Goody-Two-Shoes Jess.

'Oh no!' I thought.

Dad made me sit down and finish it, which

took ages even though there was only a little bit. Jess got to sneak in and watch a bit of the movie while I worked. Not fair!

Then Dad told both of us to get to bed. I tried to explain that I needed a little time to relax after the homework but he wouldn't listen.

Why is it that parents think you need to go to sleep early the night before a school day? You need to get every second of weekend freedom you can, can't they see that?

On Monday morning Dad woke me up. I lay there for a while thinking about this weird dream I'd had. I was being chased by hundreds of babies and my legs were weak so I couldn't get away. I was still wondering why I'd dream something like that when Mum came and hassled me until I got ready for school. She was feeling a bit sick again so I did what she asked a bit quicker than usual.

While I was putting my shoes on I tried to put some serious thinking into the Mum question.

Fifteenth Clue: Mum is sick every morning.

Something must start adding up here, if only I could could get a good run at it, I'd crack this one, I knew.

At breakfast I looked at Jess and thought about how she is different from me, apart from her being a girl I mean. She's older for a start and she thinks she knows everything, but she doesn't. Sometimes I think she's nothing like me at all.

There was definitely something going on with Mum and Dad and Jess acted as if she knew — as if! And there was that strange dream about being chased by babies.

That's when I asked Mum where babies come from. Jess heard me ask her. She laughed and said, 'Don't you know yet?'

Then she followed me when I went to ask Dad and made baby faces at me from behind him.

Dad had to go to work, but he promised he'd tell me everything I wanted to know when he came home that afternoon.

And Then It Hit Me

Before Dad came home that afternoon I decided to sit down and have a good look at the clues I'd collected about Mum and Dad's Big Secret.

There were fifteen clues, and a lot of them were about food, or Mum's stomach, or both. And she'd been sick a lot lately. This wasn't really surprising because she'd been pigging out quite a bit and also eating really weird stuff, like pickles on toast. Yuk!

Maybe she had something wrong with her stomach. Maybe she was really sick! That would explain how she knew her way around the hospital maze and how the nurse knew her. And it would explain why Dad was being extra nice to her.

Then I thought a bit longer and reckoned it couldn't be anything like that. Because why would Mum and Dad be so smug at Grandma and Grandpa's house? You don't get all pleased with yourself about being sick. And why all the maniac cleaning? That was definitely weird-o-rama.

Just then Dad came home. First he had a quiet chat with Mum — hey, this was looking mega-serious — then they both came into my room and sat down. Dad looked a bit pale and Mum looked kind of pleased. I was wondering if it was too late to change my mind about the birds and bees and escape to the backyard. Then Dad pulled some library books from behind his back, dada, like some kind of weak magic act.

He started umming and erring until Mum prodded him. It was getting to be like a weak soapy — the big moment was approaching. Then he coughed a bit and said, 'The thing is, Max, your mum and I have been expecting you to ask us about babies ... and other stuff.'

'Okay,' I thought. 'Here we go.' And I tried to look as if I wasn't bothered if he said anything else or not.

'You see, Son, when two people love each other they sometimes decide to have children together ...' and off he went on a big speech that sounded really familiar. Then I looked down at the book open on his lap and realised it was exactly the same one Tony and I found in the school library.

All the diagrams showing men's and women's bits, all labelled, and Dad was explaining all about how when a man and a woman love each other they get into all that kissy stuff, and then they ...

Man — Woman — Mum — Dad — kissy stuff —
BOOM — Baby!

Mum ... Dad ...

My head was spinning ... Mum and Dad, doing
that ... and then it dawned on me — MUM AND
DAD **DID THAT** AND **MADE ME!**

**Unbelievable! That's what happened! Un-be-
liev-able!**

But it's a fact!

My head was still spinning round and round thinking
about Mum and Dad doing **that** when Dad said, 'So
Max, your mother and I have something wonderful to
tell you.'

What could be more mind blowing than what I just
realised?

And then Jess stuck her head in the door and said,
'Hey, Factso, haven't you figured out the really big
fact yet?' in her most annoying, know-it-all voice.

WHAT FACT?

Look for other great books from Fremantle Arts Centre Press.

Whacko

Some afternoons at school are worse than being stuck upside down in a green rubbish bin with a rabid mouse down your shirt.

With five brothers and sisters, an evil nemesis and crazy parents, the last thing Jo needs is problems with the teacher. But there's trouble around every corner, and time is running out … Dead mice, foaming snails and cockroach puffing are just the start in this wacky race against the clock.

ISBN 1 86368 308 9   RRP $11.95

Destination Unknown

Vampires, robots, a dog in space, unicorns, time-travel, dragons, a griffin — you'll find all these, and more, in these unreal prize-winning stories by young writers aged from eight to thirteen.

'… it's inspiring stuff.'
Tim Winton

ISBN 1 86368 341 0   RRP $14.95

Aussie Rules!

Killer Boots

Killer boots, all right. They'd kicked some wicked goals, but Greg was worried. It'd kill him if he had to give them back, and if things went real bad, his mum would kill him too.

ISBN 1 86368 138 8   RRP $13.95

The Big Game

The Dockers have made the finals for the first time — but Greg is feeling pretty down. Then, everything starts happening. In this sequel to *Killer Boots*, footy is more than just a game, and the stakes are as high as they get.

ISBN 1 86368 183 3   RRP $13.95

Gunna Burn

The new footy season is on and Greg's dream is selection in the AFL draft, but the new coach has his own ideas and isn't listening. Meanwhile, Dockers star Matt Tognolini is on fire. The captaincy, sizzling form, high media profile, adoring fans. Can he handle the heat?

ISBN 1 86368 283 X   RRP $14.95